This Rio Chico book belongs to:

_____

THE Tumbleweed Came Back

written by
Carmela LaVigna Coyle

illustrated by
Kevin Rechin

RiO CHiCO
BOOKS FOR CHILDREN

A special thank you to talented editor Theresa Howell,
who never gave up on a story about a tumbleweed. — clvc

Rio Chico, an imprint of Rio Nuevo Publishers®
P. O. Box 5250, Tucson, AZ 85703-0250
(520) 623-9558, www.rionuevo.com

Text © 2013 by Carmela LaVigna Coyle.
Illustrations © 2013 by Kevin Rechin.

Book design: David Jenney
Editorial: Theresa Howell

Production Date: June, 2013
Printed by Guangzhou Yicai Printing Co., Ltd., Guangzhou, China
Job # J130531FC01

6   5   4   3   2   1   13   14   15   16   17   18

Library of Congress Cataloging-in-Publication Data

Coyle, Carmela LaVigna.
  The tumbleweed came back / by Carmela LaVigna Coyle.
          p. cm.
  Summary: When tumbleweeds invade Granny's house, the family pitches in to try and get rid of them but whether they are packed in a trunk and dropped in the Rio Grande or put on a train to the coast, the prickly plants keep coming back.
  ISBN 978-1-933855-83-7
  [1. Stories in rhyme. 2. Tumbleweeds—Fiction. 3. Tall tales.] I. Title.
  PZ8.3.C8396Tum 2013
  [E]—dc23
                          2012035934

For my two and only, Nick and Annie
— clvc

To my sister, Kris, for her constant inspiration
—K. R.

Amighty wind blew in
as we sat to eat our lunch.
It plopped a tiny tumbleweed
into our jug of punch.
My granny shouted,
**"EEEK, oh me!
A prickly, wicked weed!"**
So we flicked it back into the breeze
before it dropped a seed.

But the tumbleweed came back
the very next day.
Even more came back!
They just wouldn't stay away.

Rolling in the garden
and rolling past the gate,
and Granny was becoming
even more and more irate.

So we captured up the wicked weeds
and stuffed them in a trunk,
then dropped it in the Rio Grande
and watched until it sunk.
We happily reported back,
"The weeds are finally **GONE!**"
But we kept on guard into the night
and all the way till dawn.

But the tumbleweeds came back
the very next day.
Even more came back!
They just wouldn't stay away.

Hopping on the picket fence
and rolling up the stoop.
Rolling in, and rolling through,
then out the chicken coop.

We dragged all seventeen of them
    on top of Granny's shed,
then tied them to balloons
    and let them loose above our heads.
They lifted up and sailed away
    like a carnival parade,
and disappeared into the West
    as day began to fade.

But the tumbleweeds came back the very next day.
Even more came back!
They just wouldn't stay away.

Zooming toward the old red barn
    and through the double doors,
past the cow, up the loft,
    and out the second floor!

We conjured up another plan
to end the tumbleweeds.
A one-way ticket to the coast
would surely do the deed.
We boarded them onto a train
and locked the freight door tight,
and listened as the train whistle
dissolved into the night.

But the tumbleweeds came back
the very next day.
Even more came back!
They just wouldn't stay away.

Splashing in our swimming pool
and sunning on the deck,
dropping seeds on everything.
Our granny was a wreck.

We crammed them in a shipping box
    with **NO** return address,
slapped a mailing label on,
    and sent them UPS.
We woooed and hoooed, and jumped high-five.
    The weeds were gone at last!
But you'd think we'd wait to celebrate,
    until more time had passed...

'Cause tumbleweeds came back the very next day.
Even more came back! They just wouldn't stay away.
Sliding down the chimney and marching through the halls,
barging in on Granny's club, and crawling up the walls!

So we found some gears,
    a rope, and wood,
    and built a time machine,
then sent them in a capsule
    to three thousand and fifteen.
We stood beside our new gizmo,
    and grinned from ear to ear.
There was **NO** way they'd travel back
    to this exact same year.

But the tumbleweeds came back
   the very next day.
Even more came back!
   They just wouldn't stay away.

Rolling toward the closet door,
   and down the laundry chute;
socks and undies everywhere,
   they didn't give a hoot!

So we loaded up those tumbleweeds
    onto a rocket ship,
and blasted them to outer space
    for an interstellar trip.
Granny threw a victory party,
    inviting folks we know.
We sang and danced and ate until...

a wind began to blow...

A sudden hush came over us
as we ran out to see
if tumbleweeds were blowing back
from a distant galaxy.
We turned our heads toward the sky
and, much to our delight,
from here to there and in between,
no tumbleweeds in sight!